Eliza Fenwick

The Bad family

And other stories

Eliza Fenwick

The Bad family
And other stories

ISBN/EAN: 9783744750059

Printed in Europe, USA, Canada, Australia, Japan

Cover: Foto ©Andreas Hilbeck / pixelio.de

More available books at **www.hansebooks.com**

No. III.   THE BAD FAMILY.
BY MRS. FENWICK.

The Bad Family;

& Other Stories

BY

MRS. FENWICK

LONDON: GRANT RICHARDS
1898

CONTENTS

Introduction

Mrs. FENWICK, like Mrs. Turner
(some of whose Cautionary Stories
have already been published in this
series), lived and wrote at the be-
ginning of this century. Mrs.
Turner practised verse, Mrs. Fenwick prose. I can tell nothing of
Mrs. Fenwick's life, except that
among her books were *Infantine
Stories*, the *Life of Carlo, Mary and
her Cat, Presents for Good Boys and
Girls, Rays from the Rainbow* (an
easy system of teaching grammar),
and *Lessons for Children; or, Rudi-*

Introduction

ments of Good Manners, Morals, ana Humanity. It is from the last-named book that the first ten of the following stories have been taken. It was a favourite work in its day, and not only was it often reprinted in England, but was translated into French: for little French children, it seems, need lessons too.

As for these *Rudiments*, although it was Mrs. Fenwick's purpose that they should lead to good conduct, it would satisfy their present editor to know that they had amused. That is why they are printed here, and also to show the kind of reading prepared for the childhood of our great-grandmothers and great-grandfathers. In those days exaggeration was rather in favour

Introduction

with story-tellers; and we therefore need not believe that there
was ever a family quite so bad as
the Bad Family in this book, or a
Good Family so good; or that Mrs.
Loft (in 'The Basket of Plumbs')
would have bought fruit from a
household down with fever; or that
a boy of ten could write so well as
the hero of 'The Journal.' But after
making allowances for exaggeration,
we may take everything else as truth.
As I said, these stories are included
in this series chiefly to provide enter-
tainment; but if they also have the
use Mrs. Fenwick wished—if the
misadventures of Frank Lawless
keep us from robbing orchards,
and 'The Broken Crutch' leads
to the befriending of weary and

Introduction

wooden-legged sailors—why, so
much the better.

The last two stories in this book,
'Limby Lumpy' and 'The Oyster
Patties,' were not written by Mrs.
Fenwick; but they seem to fit in
here rather well.

E. V. LUCAS.

October 1898.

The Bad Family

The Bad Family

THERE is a certain street in a certain town (no matter for its name) in which there are two handsome houses of equal size. The owners of these houses have each six children, and the neighbours have named one the BAD FAMILY, and the other the GOOD FAMILY.

In the Bad Family there are three boys and three girls ; and the servants, who are always much teased and vexed when they live where there are naughty children, speak of them thus :—the eldest they call FIGHTING HARRY, the second GREEDY GEORGE, and the

The Bad Family

youngest IDLE RICHARD; the eldest
girl is nicknamed CARELESS FANNY,
the next LYING LUCY, and the
youngest SELFISH SARAH.

MASTER HENRY indeed well deserves his title, for he thinks it a
mighty fine thing to be a great
boxer, and takes great pride and
pleasure in having a black eye or a
bloody nose. This does not proceed
from courage; no, no: courage
never seeks quarrels, and is only
active to repel insult, protect the
injured, and conquer danger; but
Harry would be one of the first to
fly from real danger, or to leave the
helpless to shift for themselves. He
knows that he is very strong, and
that few boys of his age can match
him, so he picks quarrels on purpose
to fight, because his great strength
and his constant practice make him
almost sure to conquer. All his

The Bad Family

schoolfellows hate him, for such a boy can neither have a good temper, a good heart, nor good manners. It is a pity he should be sent to school, for learning is thrown away upon him ; he will be fit only to live with men that sweep the streets or drive carts and waggons, for with such coarse and vulgar habits, gentlemen will not endure him in their company.

GEORGE, the second boy, is always thinking of eating and drinking. He follows the cook from place to place to know what nice things she has got in her pantry. When there is any dainty on the dinner-table, his greedy eyes are fixed on it from the moment he sits down till he is helped, and then he grudges every morsel that any one else puts in his mouth. In his eagerness to get more than his proper share, he

The Bad Family

crams great pieces into his mouth until he is almost choked and the tears are forced from his eyes. He will get slily into the store-room and steal honey, sugar, or raisins ; and in the pantry he picks the edges of the tarts and pies, and does a number of other mean tricks. When there is company at dinner, he watches the parlour-door till they leave it, and before the servants have time to clear the table, he sips up all the drops of wine that are left in the glasses, and will even eat the parings of apples and pears that lie on the dessert plates. If he has an orange or a cake, he runs into some dirty hole to eat it, for fear his brothers and sisters should ask for a piece. If he has any money given him, he spends it all at once, and crams and eats till he can scarcely move.

The Bad Family

This greedy boy is always watched and suspected. No one will trust him in a garden, for he would eat till he made himself sick, or tear down the branches of the trees to get at the fruit. Nor can he be allowed to pay any visits, for the manners of a glutton give great offence to all well-bred people. He has a sallow, ugly look, and is always peeping and prying about, like a beast watching for its prey.

IDLE RICHARD, the third son of the Bad Family, is a great dunce. Yet he is very capable of learning well, if he chose to take the trouble, but he is fond of idleness and of nothing else. In the morning when he is called, though he knows it is time to get up, he will lie still, and after he has been called again and again, he is never ready in time for breakfast. At

The Bad Family

his meals he lolls upon the table, or against the back of his chair, and is just as slow and drawling in his manner of eating as in his learning. When he is sent to school, instead of looking at his book, he is gazing all round the room, or cutting bits of stick with his knife; sometimes he lays his head down on the desk and falls asleep, and then pretends to have the headache to excuse his idleness. His master is obliged often to punish him, and then for an hour or two he will learn very well, but next day he gets back to all his idle tricks, and does nothing; so that he is far below many boys that are much younger than himself. When other children go to play, he sits still or lies down upon the ground; he can take no pleasure, for he hates the trouble of moving, and there he sits yawning and pining for want of something to do. When he walks, he drags his feet along as if they were too heavy to lift up. His clothes are always dirty, for he will not brush them; his eyes are dull and heavy; he looks like a clown and speaks like a blockhead. Idle Richard is a burthen to himself, and scorned by everybody.

Miss Fanny has got the title of Careless, because she minds no one thing that she ought. If she goes out to walk, she is sure to lose one of her gloves, or lets her bonnet blow off into the mud, or steps into the middle of some filthy puddle, because she is staring about and not minding which way she goes. At home, when she should go to work, her needle-book, or her thimble, or her scissors cannot be found;

The Bad Family

though she has a work-basket to put these things in, they are never in the right place.

At dinner she does not observe how her plate stands on the table, and perhaps her meat and all the gravy tumble into her lap. If she has a glass of wine, she spills it on her frock ; if she hands a plate of bread and butter to any one, she is sure either to drop the plate, or to let the bread and butter fall upon the carpet. She wears very coarse clothes, for she cannot be trusted with good ones. At night when she undresses to go to bed, she throws her frock on a chair or the ground, instead of folding it neatly up, so that it is tumbled and not fit to put on the next morning. If she writes, she throws the ink about her clothes ; if she tears a hole in her frock, she does not take a

needle and thread to mend it
directly, but pins it up ; then perhaps the pin pricks her half a dozen
times in an hour, and tears three or
four more holes in the frock. It
she has a book lent to her, she will
let it fall in the dirt, or drop the
grease of the candle upon the leaves.
She is always a slattern and always
dirty ; she is a disgrace to herself
and a burthen to her friends.

What a shocking name the next
is—LYING LUCY! It is dreadful
to think that any one should deserve
to be so called, but this wicked
little girl deserves it, for she has no
sense of honour, and seldom speaks
the truth. Even when she does
say what is true, on account of her
having told falsehoods so long,
people know not how to believe
her, for who can depend upon the
word of a LIAR? If she would

The Bad Family

forbear for a whole month to tell a lie, there would be hopes of her amendment, and then her word might be taken. But till she leaves off this shameful practice, she must expect to be shunned and pointed at with scorn wherever she goes.

SELFISH SARAH loves no one but herself, and no one loves her. She will not let her brothers or sisters or any other child play with her toys, even if she is not using them. She hoards up her playthings, and cannot amuse herself with them, for fear another should touch them. If she has more sweet cake or fruit than she can eat, she puts it by, and lets it spoil and get mouldy rather than give it away ; or if she sees a poor child begging in the streets, without shoes, stockings, or clothes to cover him, she will not part with a halfpenny to buy him a

The Bad Family

bit of bread, though she is told that he is starving with hunger. She never assists any one, nor is ever thankful or grateful for what is done for her. She covets everything she sees, yet takes no real pleasure in anything.

The parents of these odious children never look happy, nor enjoy comfort. The brothers and sisters never meet but to quarrel, so that the house is always in an uproar. All abuse each other's vices, yet take no pains to cure their own faults. The servants hate them, the neighbours despise them, and the house is shunned as though it had some dreadful distemper within. They live without friends ; for no prudent persons will suffer their children to visit where they can learn nothing but wickedness and ill manners.

The Good Family

15

The Good Family

WHAT a different picture the other house presents to our view! The parents of the Good Family are always cheerful and happy; the children love each other and agree together; the servants are content and eager to oblige, and visitors delight to come to the house, because they pass their time there with both pleasure and profit.

MANLY EDWARD, the eldest son, is a fine youth, who makes himself the friend and protector of his younger brothers and sisters. Edward has true courage, for he will meet danger to help the helpless,

The Good Family

to rescue the oppressed, or in defence of the injured; yet he tries to avoid all quarrels, and is very often the peacemaker among those who are engaged in a dispute. His manners are gentle and graceful. He shuns the company of the rude vulgar boys, yet insults no one by seeming to hold them in contempt. It is not fine clothes or money that he pays respect to, it is virtue and good manners; and if the poorest boy in the school has the most of these good qualities, he gains the most of Manly Edward's love and esteem.

STUDIOUS ARTHUR, the second son of the Good Family, does not learn quickly, but what he wants of that power he makes up by diligence. As he finds he cannot get his task by heart as fast as some other boys, he therefore fixes his whole thoughts

The Good Family

on his book ; and no calls to go to play, nor any sort of thing, can draw him from his lesson till he has learned it perfectly. Arthur is seldom seen without a book in his hand ; and if he goes out to walk, he puts one in his pocket, to be ready if he should chance to have a few minutes to himself. He never wastes any time, and by that means he gains a great deal of knowledge. He is so attentive that he never forgets what he reads and learns. Arthur will, no doubt, become a very wise man, and already he often finds the knowledge he has gained of great use to him. His parents commend him, his friends admire him, and his schoolfellows respect him.

WELL-BRED CHARLES, the third son, is also a charming boy. He is greatly remarked for his perfect

The Good Family

good manners. He never forgets to behave with politeness wherever he is. In the company of his parents and their friends he is attentive to supply the wants of every one. He listens to the discourse, and when he is spoken to he answers at once in a lively, ready, and pleasant manner, but is never forward and talkative. When he has a party of playfellows, his mirth is not noisy and boisterous. He does not think, as some rude children do, that all play consists in screaming, shouting, tearing clothes, and knocking things to pieces, but finds plenty of sport for his little visitors without doing any of these things, and makes them as merry as possible. When cakes or fruit are sent into the playroom, he helps his guests all round before he touches any himself. He places them in the seats nearest the fire, or, in fine weather, where they can see the most pleasant prospect. As good manners always arise from a good temper and a kind heart which desires to make others happy, so they are sure to promote good-humour and happiness. The play-parties of Charles, therefore, are never spoilt by disputes and quarrels. His visitors come with delight, and leave him with regret.

WELL-BRED CHARLES is constantly attentive to the ease and comfort of those about him. He pays great respect and deference to people who are old. He never uses coarse words nor bad language, and always speaks civilly to servants. He does not enter the parlour with dirty hands and face, nor ever greases his clothes, for he knows that dirty habits are offensive, dis-

The Good Family

gusting things, and therefore he carefully avoids them.

Some children put on their good manners with their best clothes, and think they need behave well only before company ; but the politeness of such children is stiff, awkward, and troublesome, and they always forget themselves, and return to some of their vulgar habits, before they leave the company. It is the constant practice of good manners, at all times and in all places, that renders them easy, becoming, sweet and natural, like those of Well-bred Charles.

The daughters of this good and happy family are no less worthy of praise than the sons. The eldest girl, whom we may call PATIENT EMMA, has the misfortune to suffer from illness. Sometimes she has severe pain, yet she bears it with patience and fortitude. She even tries to hide what she feels, that she may not afflict her kind parents; and the instant she has a little ease she becomes as cheerful as any one. She submits without a murmur to take what medicines the doctors prescribe for the cure of her illness. She is not so foolish as to expect to find a pleasant taste in physic, but she expects that it will be of service to her; and she would rather have a bitter taste in her mouth for a few moments, than endure days, weeks, and months of pain and sickness. As peevish, fretful tempers often bring disease on the body, so a patient, even temper not only lessens all suffering, but helps to cure the diseases of the body; Miss Emma, therefore, will perhaps in a short time regain her health, and should such an event happen, what

The Good Family

joy it will give to all who know, pity, and admire this excellent little girl !

GENEROUS SUSAN thinks all day long how she can add to the happiness of others. It is her greatest pleasure to relieve distress, to do good, and to promote the comforts of all around her. She watches the looks of her parents, that she may fly to oblige them. If they are going out to ride in the coach, and there is not room enough for all the children, she will give up her place, that one of her brothers or sisters may go. She will at all times leave play, or decline paying a visit, to attend on Emma, her sick sister. She sits whole hours by her bedside to watch her while she sleeps, and is careful to stir neither hand or foot, lest she should disturb her slumbers. When awake, she reads to her, talks to her, or sings to her,

The Good Family

if that seems most to amuse her. She would gladly bear the pain herself, if it were possible so to relieve poor Emma.

When Susan has any money given to her, she does not treat herself with sweetmeats or toys, but buys something that will be useful to her brothers or sisters. At other times she will buy a pair of shoes for a poor child that goes barefooted, or purchase a book for some little boy or girl to learn to read in. Her mamma often gives her old frocks and gowns to bestow on some distressed family, and then Susan works with all her might for several days, to mend and make them up in the most useful manner : for she has been told that a poor woman who has two or three children to take care of, and goes out to daily labour, has not time to work with

The Good Family

her needle, and perhaps does not know how to do it properly. When Susan has mended or made three or four little frocks, and sees the children neatly dressed in them, she feels more delight and pleasure than if she had twenty dolls of her own, clothed in silks and satins. Generous Susan has the blessing or the poor and the love of all her family.

MERRY AGNES, the youngest child of the whole, is a fine, healthy, lively, sprightly, laughing little girl, who feels no pain, and has no cause for sorrow. She is a kind of plaything for her elder brothers and sisters, who all delight in her good-humour. They never tease, torment, and try to put her out of temper, as some children do to those who are younger than themselves, but they commend her good-

The Good Family

ness and strive to improve her.
When they tell her not to do
anything, she obeys them at once :
for she sees that they are all gay,
smiling, happy children, because
they do what is right. If she
wants to have what is not proper
for her, she can bear to be denied,
and skips away just as merry as
before. This little girl will become very clever, for her brothers
and sisters take pleasure in teaching
her what they have been taught,
and she attends to their lessons,
and improves by their advice. She
knows that they are all good, and
she wishes to be like them.

It is a fine sight to see this Good
Family all together : for among
them there are no sour looks or
rude words, no murmurs, no complaints, or quarrels. No : all is
kindness, peace, and happiness.

Foolish Fears

29

Foolish Fears

MARY CHARLOTTE had a silly habit of screaming when she saw a spider, an earwig, a beetle, a moth, or any kind of insect ; and the sound of a mouse behind the wainscot of the room made her suppose she should die with fright. The persons with whom she lived used to pity her for being afraid, and that made her fond of the silly trick, so that she became worse daily, and kept the house in a constant tumult and uproar : for she would make as much noise about the approach of a poor insect not much larger than the head of a pin, as if she had seen half a dozen

31

Foolish Fears

hungry wolves coming with open jaws to devour her.

Mary Charlotte was once asked by Mrs. Wilson, a very good lady, to go with her into the country, and Mary was much pleased at the thought of going to a house where there was a charming garden and plenty of nice fruit. But the country is a sad place for people who encourage such foolish fears, because one cannot walk in a garden or field without seeing numbers of harmless insects.

Mrs. Wilson, with her coach full of guests, arrived at her country-house just before dinner, and as soon as that meal was over, Mary begged leave to go out into the shrubbery. It was a charming place, and Mary was quite delighted with the clusters of roses and all the sweet-smelling shrubs and flowers that seemed to perfume the air. But as she was tripping along, behold on a sudden a frog hopped across the path. It was out of sight in a moment, yet Mary could go no farther; she stood still and shrieked with terror. At the same instant she saw a slug creeping upon her frock, and she now screamed in such a frantic manner that her cries reached the house. The company rushed out of the dining parlour, and the servants out of the kitchen. Mrs. Wilson was foremost, and in her haste to see what was the matter, she stumbled over a stone, and fell with such violence against a tree, that it cut her head dreadfully; she was covered with a stream of blood, and was taken up for dead.

It was soon known that the sight of a frog and a slug was all that

Foolish Fears

ailed Miss Mary, and then how angrily and scornfully did every one look at her, to think that her folly had been the cause of such a terrible disaster. Mary Charlotte had not a bad heart, and when she heard Mrs. Wilson's groans of pain while the doctors were dressing her wounds, she wept bitterly, and sorely repented her silly unmeaning fears.

Mrs. Wilson was in great danger for many days, and Mary crept about the house in the most forlorn manner, for no one took any notice of her, and she dared not go out in the garden, for fear still of meeting some mighty monster of a snail, or something equally alarming. At length Mrs. Wilson grew better, and then she sent for Mary to her room, and talked to her very kindly and very wisely on the folly of fearing things which had not the power to hurt her, and which were still more afraid of her than she could be of them—and with reason, since she was stronger, and had far more power to hurt and give pain than a thousand frogs or mice had.

Mary promised that she would try to get the better of her fault, and she soon proved that her promise was sincere.

One day she was with Mrs. Wilson in her chamber, and this good lady, being fatigued and sleepy, gave Mary a book of pretty stories to divert her, and begged the little girl would make no noise while she slept. Mrs. Wilson lay down on the bed, and Mary sat on a stool at some little distance. All was as still as possible. After some time, as Mary chanced to lift her

eyes from her book, she saw not
far from her a spider, who was
spinning his web up and down
from the ceiling. She was just
going to scream, when she thought
of the mischief she had already
done to Mrs. Wilson, and she for-
bore. At the same moment, as she
turned her head to the other side,
a little gray mouse sat on the table,
nibbling some crumbs of sweet cake
that had been left there. Mary
now trembled from head to foot,
but she had so much power over
herself that she neither moved nor
cried out. This effort, though it
cost her some pain at first, did her
good, for in a minute or two she
left off trembling. Her fear went
away by degrees, and then she
could observe and wonder at the
curious manner in which the spider
spun long lines of thread out of

Foolish Fears

its own mouth, and made them fast to each other and the wall just as he pleased; and could also admire the sleek coat and bright eyes of the little gray mouse on the table. Mary's book slipped from her lap, and as she stooped to catch it, that it might not fall on the floor, she was seen by the two visitors, who instantly fled away to their retreats in the greatest fright possible. Neither spider nor gray mouse appeared again that day ; and ever after Mary Charlotte had courage and prudence, and took care not to do mischief to others, nor deprive herself of pleasure, by the indulgence of foolish fears.

The Broken Crutch

The Broken Crutch

ONE hot day in the month of June, a poor sunburnt lame sailor, with but one leg, was going along the road, when his crutch broke in half, and he was forced to crawl on his hands and knees to the side of the road, and sit down to wait till some coach or cart came by, whose driver he would ask to take him up. The first that passed that way was a stage coach, but the man who drove it was a surly fellow, and he would not help the sailor, as he thought he should not be paid for it.

Soon after this the tired sailor fell fast asleep upon the ground, and though a thick shower of rain came on, yet still he slept : for sailors when on board their ships have to bear all sorts of weather.

When the wind blows, the waves of the sea often dash over the deck of the vessel and wet the poor men to the skin while they are pulling the ropes and shifting the sails.

When the lame sailor awoke he found a boy's coat and waistcoat laid on his head and shoulders, to keep him from being wet ; and the boy sat by, in his shirt, trying to mend the broken crutch with two pieces of wood and some strong twine. 'My good lad,' said the sailor, 'why did you pull off your own clothes to keep me from being wet ?' 'O,' said he, 'I do not mind the rain, but I thought the large drops that fell on your face would awake you, and you must be

The Broken Crutch

sadly tired to sleep so sound upon the bare ground. See, I have almost mended your crutch, which I found broke; and if you can lean on me, and cross yonder field to my uncle's farmhouse, I am sure he will get you a new crutch. Pray, do try to go there. I wish I was tall enough to carry you on my back.'

The sailor looked at him with tears in his eyes, and said, 'When I went to sea five years ago, I left a boy behind me, and if I should now find him such a good fellow as you seem to be, I shall be as happy as the day is long, though I have lost my leg and must go on crutches all the rest of my life.'

'What was your son's name?' the boy asked.

'Tom White,' said the sailor, 'and my name is John White.'

The Broken Crutch

When the boy heard these names he jumped up, threw his arms round the sailor's neck, and said, 'My dear, dear father, I am Tom White, your own little boy.'

How great was the sailor's joy thus to meet his own child, and to find him so good to those who wanted help! Tom had been taken care of by his uncle while his father was at sea, and the sunburnt, lame sailor found a happy home in the farmhouse of his brother; and though he had now a new crutch, he kept the broken one as long as he lived, and showed it to all strangers who came to the farm, as a proof of the kind heart of his dear son Tom.

The Journal ; or,
Birthday Gifts

The Journal ; or Birthday Gifts

IT was the custom of Mr. Clayton to present gifts to his children on their birthdays, and his gifts were of less or greater value, according to their industry, improvement, and good conduct during the year. It was also the wish of Mr. Clayton that his eldest son and daughter should each keep a journal of all their actions. He did not desire to see this journal himself, but he advised them to read over at the end of each week what they had written, that the record of what was good might incite them to other acts of virtue, and the history of their mistakes and errors serve as a warning for the future.

This kind, indulgent father seldom had cause to punish his children ; they were indeed very good and docile children, always respecting the commands of their parents, and loving each other with the true fondness of brothers and sisters.

One only of these children went to school, and that was the eldest boy, Laurence Clayton. The others were instructed by a governess at home. Laurence was a fine boy, the hope and pride of his family. For nine birthdays he had received gifts from the hand of his father as the reward of his good conduct, and now his tenth birthday was approaching, and Mr. Clayton had

Birthday Gifts

heard so pleasing an account of Laurence from his schoolmaster, that he said, beside the present he meant to give him, he would on the birthday grant any favour Laurence should ask of him.

A week only was wanting to complete Laurence's tenth year. Company was invited, and the young folks were all thinking and talking of the expected pleasures of that day—all but Laurence, who became pensive and silent, shunned his brothers and sisters, and even the presence of his father, to shut himself up in his own room ; but, as he replied, when asked about his health, that he was very well, it was supposed that he was busy at his studies, and they still prepared for the birthday.

On the 24th of August Laurence was ten years old, and a finer

E
49

morning than it proved was never seen. The two families that were invited came to breakfast. All were assembled in the parlour, and admiring a very handsome pair of globes, which, mounted on mahogany stands, were to be presented to Laurence; when he entered the room, not dressed in the suit of clothes that had been laid in his chamber, but in his oldest jacket, his cheeks quite pale, and his eyes red and swelled with weeping. He turned his head away as he passed the globes, and, dropping on his knees before his father, he said, ' O, sir, you promised to grant me a favour this day, pray let it be your forgiveness ! I know I do not deserve your pardon, but if you will forgive me this once, I am sure I never, never can deceive you again.'

Birthday Gifts

Mr. Clayton, shocked and surprised, desired to know what fault he had committed, when Laurence took his journal - book from his pocket and gave it into his father's hand, saying, 'I am ashamed to repeat what I have done, but it is written there, sir.' Mr. Clayton took the book, and told Laurence to withdraw till he had read it. On opening the journal Mr. Clayton found that all was regular down to the entry for the 2nd of August, which ran thus :—

Monday, August 2nd.—Being a school holiday, I went out with my father in a boat. He taught me to steer the rudder, while he managed the oars. It was a happy day. We dined at Mr. Black's, whose son showed me some fine drawings from busts of heathen gods, goddesses, and heroes; and my aunt Eleanor, who was there, gave me five shillings to buy Baldwin's *Pantheon*, that I might read the history of Jupiter, Juno, Mars, Minerva, Venus, Bacchus, Apollo, Hercules, and all the rest of the Pagan deities. Coming home, my father praised me for behaving well. Indeed it was a happy day.'

From the happy day Laurence had thus described, there was an entire blank in the journal ; but between the leaves was placed a written paper, from which Mr. Clayton read as follows :—

'August 23rd.—To-morrow is my birthday, and my father is preparing gifts for me, which he thinks I deserve. My brothers and sisters are rejoicing, but I am wretched ; when my father smiles on me, I feel my cheeks burn, and my heart swells as if it would burst; and when he calls me his dear good Laurence, something rises in my throat, and seems about to choke me. If these are the feelings that belong to guilt, I wonder any one can bear the pain of being wicked : for no headache or toothache ever gave me a quarter of the torment I have suffered since I became a wicked boy. Oh, my dear, kind father, take pity on me, and this once forgive me. I will tell you truly all I have done.

'On Tuesday, August 3rd, sir, I set out to go to school. It was the day after I had been so happy with you in the boat and at Mr. Black's, and as I met William Thompson, I could not help telling him what a pleasant day I had spent. "Oh, then," said he, "you are fond of the water; I and two or

three more are just going to take a
little row, and you shall go with us."
At first I refused, but William told
me I was too early for school, and
as he was also going to school, and
promised to be back in time, I at
last consented.

'Three dirty boys were waiting
at the side of the river, and though
I did not like their company, I was
then ashamed to go back, so we all
jumped into a boat and rowed
away. For some time we went on
very well ; both wind and tide were
in our favour, and it was quite easy
to manage the boat.

'The fine day and the pleasant
river soon made me forget school,
till I heard some distant clock
strike twelve ; then, distressed at
what I had done, I insisted we
should go back. But it was very
hard to row against wind and tide,

Birthday Gifts

and they began to quarrel and were going to fight. I sprang up to snatch the oar from a boy who was going to strike another, and in suddenly raising my arm I knocked his hat off into the river. It swam away, and as we were turning to row after it, we dropped one of the oars, and trying to row with the other, we ran the boat aground upon a bank of mud. There we were obliged to stay, for we could not force the boat off, nor could we wade to the shore through that mud. I bore the blame of these misfortunes; they all abused me sadly, and the boy whose hat was lost, cried and sobbed most bitterly : for, he said, he belonged to a cruel master, and should be beaten almost to death; so at last, to make him quiet, I promised to give him mine.

The Journal ; or,

'Well, sir, there we stayed, and
I heard the same clock strike one,
two, three, and four. At last, two
men called to us from the opposite
side of the river. They were the
owners of the boat we had taken
away, and were in search of it.
They got another boat, and came
to us in a great passion, swearing
that if we did not pay them
five shillings each for the day's
work we had hindered them of,
and pay for the oar we had lost,
they would take us before a justice
of the peace and have us sent to
prison. William Thompson had
no money in his pocket, but I
had the five shillings my Aunt
Eleanor had given me the day
before at Mr. Black's to buy the
Pantheon; that they took, but not
being enough to satisfy their de-
mand, they also took away my

satchel with all my school books,
telling me where they lived, and
that they would restore it safe as
soon as I brought them the rest of
the money. The other boys were
so poor and so ragged, the men
did not ask anything of them.

'It was near six o'clock when
we got on shore, about the time I
knew I should be expected home
from school. William Thompson
went down on his knees to beg I
would not tell what had happened,
promising at the same time to bring
the money to release my books the
next morning. Indeed I was so
much ashamed of having played
truant thus, that I was glad enough
to conceal it. The boy whose
hat I had knocked off into the river
would not leave me till he had got
mine, so I was forced to slip in
at the garden-gate and steal up the

back stairs to my own room, that I might not be seen to come home without my hat. I was now very hungry, yet afraid to show myself; when I was called to tea, my legs trembled under me as I went downstairs. I met my sister Molly in the hall, who gave me an apple, and then asked me what I had had for dinner at school. I turned from her, for I knew not what to answer; but as soon as I got into the parlour, you, sir, told me to bring you my Latin grammar. Then I was forced to answer, and a lie seemed easier than the truth : so I said I had left my satchel and my books at school. I could not play nor amuse myself any way all that evening, and when I took up my journal, what had I to set down—that I had played truant, lost my hat and my money, and told my father a lie? No, no, I could not bear to write all that.

'Next morning, sir, I had new troubles. I was forced to steal slyly out of the house, that no one might see me put on my best hat, and when I got to William Thompson's, he had got no money to give me. I dared not go to school without my books, so I went to seek the man that had them. He was gone to his daily work, and we could not find him, and I waited and loitered till he came home to his dinner. I begged and prayed for my books, and at last he gave them up to me, making me promise I would bring him the money next day, or something that he could sell for money, which if I did not do, he said he would come and declare the whole story to you, sir. I got to school that day time enough for afternoon's

lessons, and was forced to tell another lie to my master, to excuse
my not coming sooner.

'I had no dinner either that day ;
but the pain of hunger was nothing
to the fear of being found out.
Well, sir, to tell all the worst at
once, I have from time to time
carried away, to pay the man whose
oar we had lost, my silver pen and
pencil, my compasses, my pocket
inkstand, and that handsome bound
set of Natural History you gave me
on my last birthday. Then in
going to seek him, I have stayed
away three more mornings from
school. And my head has been so
filled with other thoughts that I
have not minded my lessons as I
used to do. I have lost my place
in my class twice, have been
punished once, and my master
threatens to make complaints to

Birthday Gifts

you, sir, of the change in my conduct. To excuse wearing my best
hat, I did also invent a wicked lie
of having lost my other at school.

'Alas! alas! how many sad
things have I been guilty of since
I first played truant! If I had but
confessed my fault that day, how
many more I should have avoided!
I have never known a happy moment
since, and if I could describe to my
brothers and sisters the pain and
grief I have felt, I am sure they
would never be as naughty as I
have been.

'O, sir, I cannot bear to deceive
you any longer, and if you will
grant me your pardon, indeed, indeed, I will try never to offend you
more.'

It is not possible to express how
great Mr. Clayton's surprise and
sorrow was on perusing this paper;

yet, convinced by Laurence's candid confession of his faults that his penitence was sincere, he consented to forgive him the past and restore him to his favour. Laurence knelt at his father's feet, and while he kissed his parent's hand and bathed it in tears of gratitude, he felt the first moment of pleasure he had known for three long weeks.

Though all were glad to see Laurence forgiven, no one could be merry ; and it was the first grave birthday that had ever been known in the family. The globes were covered up and sent into Mr. Clayton's library : for though he could forgive, it would not have been right to have rewarded Laurence, as if he had not done wrong. But that day twelvemonth came, and then Laurence deserved the globes and the love and praise of every

Birthday Gifts

one for his diligence and goodness throughout the year. Whenever he was tempted to do wrong, he remembered that one error often becomes the source of many others, and carefully avoided committing the first fault. His journal was kept faithfully, and all the days in it were happy days; and on his eleventh birthday Laurence could play and dance with a light heart and a clear conscience.

The Basket of Plumbs

F   65

The Basket of Plumbs [1]

A POOR girl, whose face was pale
and sickly, and who led a little
ragged child by the hand, came up
one day to the door of a large house,
and, seeing a boy standing there,
said to him, 'Do, pray, sir, ask
your mamma to buy these plumbs.
There are four dozen in my basket.'
George Loft took the basket to his
mother, who counted the plumbs,
and finding them right in number
and that they were sound, good
fruit, sent out to know the price.

[1] The spelling is Mrs. Fenwick's.

The Basket of Plumbs

The girl asking more than Mrs. Loft thought they were worth, she put the plumbs again into the basket, and told George to carry them back, and say it did not suit her to buy them.

Now these plumbs were fresh picked from the tree ; they had a fine bloom on them, and were very tempting to the eye. George loved plumbs above all other fruit, and he walked very slowly from the parlour with his eyes fixed on the basket. The longer he looked, the more he wished to taste them. One plumb, he thought, would not be missed ; and as he put his hand in to take that one, two others lay close under his fingers. It was as easy to take three as one, and the three plumbs were taken and put into his pocket. When he reached the hall door and gave the basket back to the girl,

The Basket of Plumbs

his face was as red as a flame of fire, but she did not notice it, nor thought of counting her plumbs; for how could she suppose any one in *that* house would be so mean as to take from *her* little store!

It chanced that as the girl turned from the door, Mrs. Loft came to the parlour window, and, seeing the girl look so ill, she felt sorry she had not bought the plumbs. Therefore, throwing up the sash, she asked the cause of her sickly looks. The girl then told a sad story of distress: she had been ill of a fever; her parents had caught the disease of her, and were now very bad and not able to work for the support of their children. In the little garden of their cottage a plumb-tree grew, and she had picked the ripe plumbs and had come out to sell them that she might buy

The Basket of Plumbs

physic for her parents and food for
herself and her hungry little sister.
Mrs. Loft paid the girl the full
price for her plumbs, gave her wine
to carry to her sick parents and
food for herself and the child, and
bade her return the next day for
more.

Soon after the grateful girl had
left the house, Mrs. Loft, placing
the fruit in her dessert-baskets,
found that, instead of forty-eight,
there were only forty-five plumbs ;
and, far from thinking her son had
been guilty of the theft, she laid
the blame on the girl, who she now
thought had tried to impose on her.
It was not the loss of three plumbs
that Mrs. Loft cared for, but the
want of an honest mind that gave
her offence.   She had meant to be
a friend to the poor girl, but now
she began to doubt the truth of her

The Basket of Plumbs

story ; for Mrs. Loft thought if she could impose in one thing she might also in others. Deeming the girl therefore no longer worthy of her kindness, she gave orders for her to be sent away when she came on the morrow.

George had heard the whole : first, the tale of distress, and then his mother's censure of the blameless girl. He had not only taken from a poor, wretched creature a part of her little all, but had been the means of bringing a foul reproach upon her, while her parents, who might have been saved from greater distress by his mother's bounty, would now be left helpless, in sickness and in sorrow. All this cruel mischief he had done for the sake of eating three plumbs — he, too, who had never wanted food, clothes, nor anything a child need desire to possess. He felt the bitter pangs of guilt, and the fruit, whose shape and bloom had looked so tempting, was now as hateful as poison to the sight of George.

There was still a way left to make some amends: namely, to confess his fault to his mother. It did require some courage to do this; and when a boy throws away his sense of honour, no wonder his courage should forsake him. George could not resolve to disclose a crime to his mother, which he thought she never would find out. The first day in each week he had sixpence given him for pocket-money, and he laid a plan to save that money, and to bestow it for a month to come on the girl. This, he thought, was doing even more than justice : for as her three plumbs were only worth one penny, he should by this

The Basket of Plumbs

means give her two shillings for
them, and save his own credit with
his mamma. He wished with all
his heart he had never touched the
plumbs ; but as he had done it, it
seemed to him less painful to leave
the poor girl to suffer the blame,
than to accuse himself.

With this plan of further deceit
in his mind, George went to dinner;
but before the cloth was taken from
the table he had reason enough to
repent of his double error. Mrs.
Loft, in paying for the plumbs, had
given a number of half-pence,
among which, unseen by her, a
shilling had slipped. When the
poor girl reached the cottage she
found the shilling, and lost not a
moment in coming back to restore
it to its right owner. Mrs. Loft
well knew that she who could be
thus just in one instance must have

The Basket of Plumbs

an honest mind. Her doubts of the poor girl were at an end, but no sooner did she cast her eyes on George, than she read, in the deep blush that spread over his face, in his downcast look, and the trembling of his limbs, who was the guilty person.

Guilt not only fixes the stings of remorse within the bosom, but imprints its hateful mark upon the outward form.

The Choice of Friends

75

The Choice of Friends

THE moon was shining on a clear cold night, and it was near ten o'clock, and all the children of the village of Newton, except one, were in bed and asleep. That one, whose name was Frank Lawless, was above three miles from home, weeping with pain and fear, alone, forlorn, cold, and wretched, with no shelter but a leafless hedge and no seat but a hard stone ; while his father and mother were running wildly about the fields and lanes, not knowing what had become of their naughty boy.

The Choice of Friends

Frank Lawless had been playing truant that day, and was met by his father with a number of bad boys, to whom he ought not at any time to have spoken. They were the children of brickmakers, and most likely they had never been taught what was right; so that if they said wicked words, told lies, and took things which did not belong to them, one could scarcely wonder at it; but that Frank Lawless, who had the means of knowing the value of good conduct and good manners, should choose such boys for his friends and play-fellows, was indeed most strange. Yet thus it was; their shouting, laughing, and vulgar mirth pleased Frank. They had also a great share of cunning, and found the way to manage him, so as to get from him what they wanted to have. When

The Choice of Friends

they told Frank that he was very handsome and very clever, and that it was a shame so fine a boy should be forced to go to school if he did not like it, he was silly enough to be pleased, and gave them in return his playthings and his money ; nay, he would even take sugar, cakes, fruit, and sweetmeats from his mother's store-room to bestow on these ill-chosen friends ; and their false pretence of love for him made him quite careless of gaining the real love of his father and mother.

On meeting his son in the midst of the brickmakers' children, Mr. Lawless[1] was very angry, and, taking him home by force, he gave him a severe reproof, and then locked him up in his chamber. Frank,

[1] One drawback to bringing Frank's father into the story is that he, in spite of his character, has to be called Lawless too.

The Choice of Friends

who had lately grown very sullen and froward, was far from being sorry for his fault, and said to himself that his father was both cross and cruel, and wished to prevent his being happy. With these wicked thoughts in his head, he began to contrive how to make his escape ; and the window not being very high above the ground, and having a vine growing up to it, whose branches would serve as a sort of ladder, he got out, reached the ground, and passing unseen through the garden-gate, ran with all his speed till he came up to the boys, who were still at the cruel sport of robbing birds'-nests in the lane where he had left them.

But he did not seem half as welcome to them now as in the morning, when he had brought a pocket full of apples, and as he

The Choice of Friends

said he was come to live with them,
and should never go home again,
their manner was quite changed.
One took away his hat and another
his shoes. They cut sticks to make
a bonfire, and, having got a great
pile, they made Frank carry it.
The weight was too much for him,
and when he let it fall, they gave
him hard words and still harder
blows. He now began to find that
the service of the wicked is by no
means so easy as to obey the commands of the good.

   While Frank Lawless was toiling
under his heavy load of sticks, the
boys were laying a plan to rob an
orchard. It was the autumn season
of the year, and all the fruit of the
orchard was gone, except the pears
of one tree, which, as it stood very
near the dwelling-house of the
owner of the orchard, these boys

The Choice of Friends

had been afraid to climb. Now having Frank Lawless in their power, they thought of making him, in the dusk of the evening, commit the theft and run all the hazard, while they stayed in safety by the hedge, ready to receive the stolen fruit. Frank, dreading what might happen to him in the daring attempt, begged and prayed them not to force him there; but he had made himself a slave to hard task-masters, and they cuffed and kicked him, till, to escape from their hands, he climbed the tree.

Scarcely had Frank pulled half-a-dozen pears, when his false friends heard the farmer who owned the orchard come singing up the lane: and, to save themselves from being thought to have any concern with it, they began to pelt Frank with stones, and cry aloud—'*See, see, there*

The Choice of Friends

is a boy robbing Farmer Wright's pear - tree.' Frank got down as quickly as he could, but not soon enough to escape the angry farmer, who gave him a most severe horse-whipping, while those who had brought him into this sad scrape stood laughing, hooting, and clapping their hands. It was useless to try to excuse himself; he had been seen in the tree, the pears were found in his pocket, and the farmer, after whipping him without mercy, pushed him out of the orchard and bade him be gone.

Smarting now with pain, and almost blinded by his tears, he ran to get away from the false and cruel boys who were making sport of what they had caused him to suffer, when one, still more wicked than the rest, threw a great stone after him, which, hitting his ankle-

The Choice of Friends

bone, gave him such extreme torture that he sank on the ground not able to proceed a step farther. The boys made off in alarm at what they had done, and Frank, in terror and pain, sat sobbing on a stone till he was found by his father, who had been searching for him in the greatest distress.

His father took him home, warmed and fed him and healed his bruises, though after such extreme bad conduct, he could not esteem and caress him like a good child. It was happy for Frank Lawless that he took the warning of that day. He had gained nothing but shame, pain, and sorrow by his choice of wicked friends, and from that time he chose with more wisdom. Good conduct brought him back to his father's favour, and now at ten o'clock at night, when

The Choice of Friends

the moon and stars were shining in the sky, and the air was cold and frosty, Frank Lawless was always snug in bed, like the rest of the good children of the little village of Newton.[1]

[1] There is one error in this story which perhaps it is worth while to point out. Birds'-nesting and orchard-robbing are not in season together.

Cousin James and
Cousin Thomas

87

Cousin James and Cousin Thomas

JAMES BROWN was born at a farm-house. He had not seen a town or a city when he was ten years old.

James Brown rose from his bed at six in the morning during summer. The men and maids of a farmhouse rise much sooner than that hour, and go to their daily work. Some yoke the oxen to the plough, some bring the horses in from the field, some mend the hedges, some manure the land, some sow seed in the ground, and some plant young trees. Those who have the care of the sheep, and who are called shepherds, take their flocks from the fold and lead them to their pasture on the hills, or in the green meadows by the running brook. The maids meanwhile haste to milk the cows, then churn the butter, put the cheese into the cheese - press, clean their dairy, and feed the pigs, geese, turkeys, ducks, and chickens. James Brown did not work in the fields, so when he rose from his bed, his first care was to wash his face and hands, to comb and brush his hair ; and when these things were done, and he had said his morning prayers, he went with his father about the farm or weeded the garden. Garden work was very proper for a boy of his age and size.

James Brown had a cousin, named Thomas, and Thomas

Cousin Thomas

Brown once came to pay James a visit. The two boys were very glad to see each other, and Thomas told James of the famous city of London, where he lived. He spoke of the spacious paved streets, crowded all day by throngs of people, and lighted at night by rows, on each side of the way, of glass lamps. He told him of the fine toy-shops, where all kinds of playthings for children are sold: such as bats, balls, kites, marbles, tops, drums, trumpets, whips, wheel-barrows, shuttles, dolls, and baby-houses. And of other great shops where linens, muslins, silks, laces, and ribbons fill the windows, and make quite a gay picture to attract the passers-by. He described also the noble buildings and the great river Thames, with its fine arched bridges, built of stone. He spoke of the immense number of boats, barges, and vessels that sail and row upon the Thames, and of the great ships that lie at anchor there, which bring stores of goods from all parts of the world. He told him of the King's palace and the Queen's palace, of the park and the canal, with the stately swans that are seen swimming on it.

Nor did he forget to describe Saint Paul's Church, with its fine choir, its lofty dome and cupola, and its curious whispering gallery, where a whisper breathed to the wall on one side is carried round by the echo, and the words are heard distinctly on the opposite side of the gallery. He spoke also of Westminster Abbey, that fine old Gothic building which contains a great number of monuments, erected there to keep alive the remembrance

Cousin Thomas

of the actions of great and wise men.

He told James likewise of the Tower of London, which is always guarded by soldiers, and in one part of which he had seen lions, tigers, a wolf, a spotted panther, a white Greenland bear, and other wild beasts, with many sorts of monkeys.[1]

Thomas Brown talked very fast on these subjects, and as James, who had never seen anything of the kind, was quite silent, and seemed as much surprised as pleased with all that he heard, Thomas began to think his cousin was but a dull, stupid sort of boy. But the next morning, when they went out

[1] These, it is sad to say, have now gone. Beyond a venerable raven, the Tower has no live stock. To-day Thomas would describe the Zoo instead.

into the fields, he found that James
had as much knowledge as himself,
though not of the same kind.
Thomas knew not wheat from
barley, nor oats from rye ; nor did
he know the oak tree from the elm,
nor the ash from the willow. He
had heard that bread was made from
corn, but he had never seen it
threshed in a barn from the stalks,
nor had he ever seen a mill grinding
it into flour. He knew nothing of
the manner of making and baking
bread, of brewing malt and hops
into beer, or of the churning of
butter. Nor did he even know
that the skins of cows, calves, bulls,
horses, sheep, and goats were made
into leather.

James Brown perfectly knew
these, and many other things of the
same nature, and he willingly
taught his cousin to understand

some of the arts that belong to the practice of husbandry.

These friendly and observing boys, after this time, met always once a year, and they were eager in their separate stations to acquire knowledge, that they might impart it to each other at the end of the twelvemonth. So that Thomas, while living in a crowded city, gained a knowledge of farming and all that relates to a country life; and James, though dwelling a hundred miles from London, knew all the curious things that it contained.

The Disasters of
Impatience

The Disasters of Impatience

On the day that Mr. Daleham removed from his town residence to his new house in the country there was much bustle and business in the family. The servants were all employed in unpacking and arranging chairs, tables, sofas, and sideboards in their proper places. Some men were putting up beds, while others were hanging window-curtains and nailing down carpets. The only idle persons in the house were Arnold and Isabel, and they could find nothing to do but to skip from room to room, ask questions, admire their new dwelling-house, and talk of the pleasure they should receive in a visit their father was engaged to make that day to Mr. Morton, his intimate friend, who lived about one mile and a half distant.

So desirous were Arnold and Isabel of seeing Morton Park, or rather perhaps of eating some of the fine grapes and melons which they had heard grew in Mr. Morton's hot-house, that the morning seemed to be the length of the whole day. When people are without employment, time hangs heavily on their hands, and minutes will appear to be as long as hours. Half a dozen times in the course of the morning these children ran to the door of the library, to ask their father when he would be ready to go, and though he was engaged sorting papers and arranging his books, they did not forbear their troublesome inquiries till he was quite angry with them.

At length, however, the joyful tidings came to Arnold and Isabel that they were to dress directly, as their father would be ready to set out in half an hour. As the day was very fine, and the coachman's assistance was useful to the other servants busied in disposing the furniture in the various apartments, Mr. Daleham chose to walk to Morton Park; but after he had dressed, and the half-hour had elapsed, he still had orders to give that detained him.

Arnold and Isabel meanwhile were standing at the hall door, almost wild with their impatience to be gone; and at last Arnold proposed to his sister that they should go on first, as their papa could soon overtake them ; and Isabel eagerly ran to ask the housekeeper whether they must take the right or the left-hand road. The housekeeper was busy with a basket of china, some of which had been broken in the carriage ; and as her thoughts were fixed on the fragments of the china, she scarcely attended to the nature of Isabel's question, and said hastily that the right-hand road led to Morton Park ; and so it did, but that was the coach road, and Mr. Daleham meant to go a much nearer and cleaner way, upon a raised path across some pleasant meadows.

No sooner had Isabel received the housekeeper's reply than away they went, and in their eagerness to reach Morton Park, they did

Impatience

not at first observe that the lane was very dirty; but at last some large splashes of mud on Isabel's clean frock attracted Arnold's notice, and he then perceived that his own white stockings and nankeen trousers were in the same dirty state. What was now to be done? They both felt that it was highly improper to go to a gentleman's house in such a condition; but then Arnold said that his father must know that the road was dirty after so much rain as they had had lately, and as he meant to walk, he supposed their getting a few splashes was of no consequence. Isabel agreed with this mode of reasoning, and on they went, expecting every moment to hear their father's steps behind them.

The lane now became wider and more open to the beams of the

sun, which had dried the pathway ;
but though they were somewhat
out of the mud, the heat of the sun
was so intense they knew not how
to bear it, and they walked as fast
as they could in order to get to
some shady place. While they
were panting with heat, they suddenly came to a stream that ran
directly across the road, and it had
no bridge over it, because foot
passengers rarely came that way.

They were now in the greatest
distress. To stand still in the full
burning sun was dreadful, and to
go back was equally fatiguing.
There was no place to sit down in
that part of the road, but on the
opposite side of the stream three
large oak trees were growing, and
formed a pleasant shade over a
green bank. Isabel, greatly tired,
and almost fainting with heat,

wished she could get to the shady
bank; so did Arnold, and he said
he 'could take off his shoes and
stockings, and carry his sister through
the water on his back. This plan
was settled; and they agreed that,
when they were over the stream,
they would wait on the bank for
their papa, and endeavour to rub
off upon the grass the clots of mud
that stuck to their shoes. But
either Arnold was not so strong as
he had supposed he was, or Isabel,
having her brother's shoes and
stockings to carry in her hand, did
not hold fast round his neck, for
just as they were in the middle of
the stream, his foot slipped, he
staggered, fell, and down went
brother and sister at once into the
pool.

Both scrambled up in a moment,
and neither had suffered more

injury than being completely bathed in the water. With streaming hair and dripping garments they reached the bank ; but when Isabel saw that the ribbons of her new straw bonnet were spoiled, she began to cry and accuse her brother of having thrown her down on purpose, which so provoked the young gentleman, that he said it was all owing to her clumsiness, and at the same time he shook the sleeves of his jacket, from which he was wringing the wet, in her face. Isabel's anger increasing at this, she rudely gave her brother a severe box on the ear. A scuffle now ensued, which caused a second tumble, and this fall being on the rough gravel, Isabel's face was scratched by the sharp pebbles, and Arnold's elbow sadly cut by a large flint stone.

The smart of these wounds cooled

their passions; they thought no more of fighting, and were wiping away the blood, and looking with grief and dismay at their wet, dirty clothes, when a servant came up who had been sent in pursuit of them.

Mr. Daleham was not far behind. He had been told that Arnold and Isabel were gone before him, and was much alarmed at not finding them in the field-path. He had therefore returned the same way to search for them; he ordered the servant to conduct them home, and told them that their silly impatience had spoiled their pleasure, as it was not possible for them now to appear at Morton Park.

Mr. Daleham then hastened on, for fear Mr. Morton's dinner should wait for him; and Arnold and Isabel, forlorn, wet, draggled, and

Disasters of Impatience

dirty, were led back to their own house. They passed a dismal afternoon, lamenting their folly and imprudence; and next morning they heard that there were not only plenty of grapes, melons, peaches, and filberts on Mr. Morton's table, but that also a very merry party of children were assembled there, who danced on the lawn till the dusk of evening approached, and then played at blindman's buff in the great hall.

The Deaf and Dumb Boy

The Deaf and Dumb Boy

'Now, my dear boy and girl,' said their aunt to Charles and Helen Laurie, 'you are come to stay a whole fortnight with me, and we must take care not to mis-spend our time, for not all the art of man can restore one day that is lost. You, Charles, shall practise your drawing while Helen works, and then while I hear Helen spell and read, you may write. Each day of our lives should be made some good use of; and while we are young,

111

The Deaf and Dumb Boy

and have health and strength, we ought to learn all those things which we may wish to know when we are grown old.'

Charles and Helen Laurie now ran in search of their books, which were soon found, as they were laid in the right place; and then they sat down to their tasks, glad to please their aunt, and quite certain that to learn to be wise and good was the best thing in the world.

At the hour of noon, when the clock had struck twelve, their aunt told them to leave their books, put on their hats, and go out to walk with her. They went through some fields, and down a pretty lane, and in the hedges on each side were tall oak, elm, and poplar trees, that made the lane look like a grove, and kept them from the

The Deaf and Dumb Boy

rays of the sun. At length they came to a small, neat, white house that stood on a green lawn, and had bushes of lilac blossoms before the windows, with a large fish-pond at the end of it. The house had rails before it, and Charles and Helen went with their aunt through a gate that was made of the tools that men work with in the fields, such as a rake, a spade, a hoe, and a scythe.

In the house they saw a fine-looking boy of ten years of age, with light-brown hair, hazel eyes, and cheeks as red as a rose. He came up to Charles and Helen, and shook hands with them, and seemed joyous at seeing them, but did not say a word. They thought it strange that he did not speak to them ; and at last Charles said to him, 'Your lawn would be a good

The Deaf and Dumb Boy

place to play at trap-ball on, if it
were not for the fish-pond that is
so near it. Do you play at trap-
ball, sir ? '

The boy, whose name was Jackson, put his hand to his mouth,
shook his head, got up from his
chair, went for a slate, wrote on it,
and gave it to Charles, who read
these words : 'I cannot speak to
you. I do not hear what you say
to me. I am a poor deaf and dumb
boy, but I shall be glad to please
you, now you have been so kind as
to come to see me. Pray write
down on this slate what you wish
me to do.'

Charles took the slate, and when
Helen read the words that were
written on it, her eyes were full of
tears, to think that such a sweet
boy should be deaf and dumb.
But Charles hung his head, for

The Deaf and Dumb Boy

Jackson wrote so fine a hand, that he did not like to show that he could not perform as well. Helen knew what Charles was thinking of, for she had heard him found fault with, and had seen him write when he did not take pains to learn to write a fine hand; so she went to the hall door and made a sign to Jackson, as much as to say they would like to go out.

Jackson led them round the lawn to the fish-pond, and that they might see the fish, he threw in some pieces of bread to make the fish jump up to catch the bread in their mouths. He next took them to the back of the house to show them the farm-yard; there they saw cocks and hens on the rubbish heap, ducks and geese dipping or swimming in the pond, pigs grunting, cows, calves, and a pet lamb,

The Deaf and Dumb Boy

who, as soon as he saw them, came out of a barn and ran up to Jackson, that he might stroke and play with him ; but he was full of tricks, and when Charles or Helen went near him he strove to butt them with his young horns. He would not eat out of their hands, but he took all that Jackson gave him. In the same barn that the lamb came out of, were a goat and two young kids. The goat, the kids, the lamb, the calves, all were fond of Jackson, for he had a kind heart and would not hurt the smallest insect.

Charles and Helen stayed that day to dine with Jackson, of whom they grew more and more fond each moment that they were with him. He was a boy of a sweet, gentle temper, and won the kindness of all who came to his house. He drew as well as he wrote, and knew all the

The Deaf and Dumb Boy

things that a deaf and dumb boy could learn. He had a box of tools, and had made a bird-cage and a neat desk to write on. It is a sad thing to be deaf and dumb, for much of what boys learn at school, and which it is right to know, cannot be taught to a deaf and dumb child.

Charles told his aunt Laurie, as they went home at night, that when he had grown to be a man he would love Jackson, and try to be of use to him, since blind or deaf and dumb men must want some one to guide and take care of them.

It is a sad thing not to see, or not to speak and hear; so that all boys and girls who have their sight and speech should be glad to make the best use of them. They should, while they are young, do what they are told by their friends is right to

The Deaf and Dumb Boy

be done, and then when they grow up they can be of great use in the world. A fool, a dunce, or a bad man does harm and not good in the world.

Limby Lumpy

119

Limby Lumpy ;

Or, the Boy who was Spoiled by his Mamma [1]

I

LIMBY LUMPY was the only son of his mamma. His father was called the 'Pavior's Assistant'; for he was so large and heavy, that when he used to walk through the streets the men who were ramming the stones down with a large wooden rammer would say, 'Please to walk

[1] This story and the one which follows it are not by Mrs. Fenwick. 'Limby Lumpy' is from *The Holiday Book*.

121

Limby Lumpy

over these stones, sir.' And then the men would get a rest.

Limby was born on the 1st of April; I do not know how long ago; but, before he came into the world, such preparations were made. There was a beautiful cradle; and a bunch of coral, with bells on it; and lots of little caps; and a fine satin hat; and tops and bottoms for pap; and two nurses to take care of him. He was, too, to have a little chaise, when he grew big enough; after that, he was to have a donkey, and then a pony. In short, he was to have the moon for a plaything, if it could be got; and, as to the stars, he would have had them, if they had not been too high to reach.

Limby made a rare to-do when he was a little baby. But he never was a *little* baby—he was always a

Limby Lumpy

big baby ; nay, he was a big baby till the day of his death.

'Baby Big,' his mamma used to call him ; he was 'a noble baby,' said his aunt ; he was 'a sweet baby,' said old Mrs. Tomkins, the nurse ; he was 'a dear baby,' said his papa,—and so he was, for he *cost* a good deal. He was 'a darling baby,' said his aunt, by the mother's side ; 'there never was such a fine child,' said everybody, before the parents ; when they were at another place they called him 'a great, ugly, fat child.'

Limby was almost as broad as he was long. He had what some people called an open countenance ; that is, one as broad as a full moon. He had what his mamma called beautiful auburn locks, but what other people said were carroty ; not before the mother, of course.

Limby Lumpy

Limby had a flattish nose and a widish mouth, and his eyes were a little out of the right line. Poor little dear, he could not help that, and therefore it was not right to laugh at him.

Everybody, however, laughed to see him eat his pap, for he would not be fed with the patent silver pap-spoon which his father bought him ; but used to lay himself flat on his back, and seize the pap-boat with both hands, and never leave go of it till its contents were fairly in his dear little stomach.

So Limby grew bigger and bigger every day, till at last he could scarcely draw his breath, and was very ill ; so his mother sent for three apothecaries and two physicians, who looked at him, and told his mamma there were no hopes : the poor child was dying of over-

Limby Lumpy

feeding. The physicians, however, prescribed for him—a dose of castor oil.

His mamma attempted to give him the castor oil; but Limby, although he liked tops and bottoms, and cordial, and pap, and sweet-bread, and oysters, and other things nicely dished up, had no fancy for castor oil, and struggled, and kicked, and fought every time his nurse or mamma attempted to give it him.

'Limby, my darling boy,' said his mamma, 'my sweet cherub, my only dearest, do take its oily poily—there's a ducky, deary—and it shall ride in a coachy poachy.'

'O! the dear baby,' said the nurse, 'take it for nursey. It will take it for nursey—that it will.'

The nurse had got the oil in a silver medicine spoon, so contrived that if you could get it into the

Limby Lumpy

child's mouth the medicine must go down. Limby, however, took care that no spoon should go into his mouth ; and when the nurse tried the experiment for the nineteenth time, gave a plunge and a kick, and sent the spoon up to the ceiling, knocked off nurse's spectacles, upset the table on which all the bottles and glasses were, and came down whack on the floor.

His mother picked him up, clasped him to her breast, and almost smothered him with kisses. 'O ! my dear boy,' said she, 'it shan't take the nasty oil—it won't take it, the darling ; naughty nurse to hurt baby : it shall not take nasty physic'; and then she kissed him again.

Poor Limby, although only two years old, knew what he was at— he was trying to get the master of

Limby Lumpy

his mamma; he felt he had gained his point, and gave another kick and a squall, at the same time planted a blow on his mother's eye.

'Dear little creature,' said she, 'he is in a state of high convulsions and fever—he will never recover.'

But Limby did recover, and in a few days was running about the house, and the master of it; there was nobody to be considered, nobody to be consulted, nobody to be attended to, but Limby Lumpy.

II

Limby grew up big and strong; he had everything his own way. One day, when he was at dinner with his father and mother, perched upon a double chair, with his silver knife and fork, and silver mug to

127

Limby Lumpy

drink from, he amused himself by playing drums on his plate with the mug.

'Don't make that noise, Limby, my dear,' said his father. 'Dear little lamb,' said his mother, 'let him amuse himself. Limby, have some pudding?'

'No; Limby no pudding'—*drum! drum! drum!*

A piece of pudding was, however, put on Limby's plate, but he kept on drumming as before. At last he drummed the bottom of the mug into the soft pudding, to which it stuck, and by which means it was scattered all over the carpet.

'Limby, my darling,' said his mother; and the servant was called to wipe Limby's mug and pick the pudding up from the floor. Limby would not have his mug wiped, and floundered about, and upset the cruet-stand and the mustard on the table-cloth.

'O! Limby Lumpy; naughty boy,' said his father.

'Don't speak so cross to the child; he is but a child,' said his mother; 'I don't like to hear you speak so cross to the child.'

'I tell you what it is,' said his father, 'I think the boy does as he likes; but I don't want to inter-fere.'

Limby now sat still, resolving what to do next. He was not hungry, having been stuffed with a large piece of pound cake about an hour before dinner; but he wanted something to do, and could not sit still.

Presently a saddle of mutton was brought on the table. When Limby saw this he set up a crow of delight. 'Limby ride,' said he,

Limby Lumpy

'Limby ride'; and rose up in his chair, as if to reach the dish.

'Yes, my ducky, it shall have some mutton,' said his mamma; and immediately gave him a slice, cut up into small morsels. That was not it. Limby pushed that on the floor, and cried out, 'Limby on meat! Limby on meat!'

His mamma could not think what he meant. At last, however, his father recollected that he had been in the habit of giving him a ride occasionally, first on his foot, sometimes on the scroll end of the sofa, at other times on the top of the easy chair. Once he put him on a dog, and more than once on the saddle; in short, he had been in the habit of perching him on various things; and now Limby, hearing this was a *saddle* of mutton, wanted to take a ride on it.

Limby Lumpy

'Limby on—Limby ride on bone,' said the child, in a whimper.

'Did you *ever hear?*' said the father.

'What an extraordinary child!' said the mother; 'how clever to know it was like a saddle—the little dear. No, no, Limby—grease frock, Limby.'

But Limby cared nothing about a greasy frock, not he—he was used enough to that; and therefore roared out more lustily for a ride on the mutton.

'Did you ever know such a child? What a dear, determined spirit!'

'He is a child of an uncommon mind,' said his mother. 'Limby, dear — Limby, dear — silence! silence!'

The truth was, Limby made such a roaring, that neither father nor

Limby Lumpy

mother could get their dinners, and scarcely knew whether they were eating beef or mutton.

'It is impossible to let him ride on the mutton,' said his father : 'quite impossible ! '

'Well, but you might just put him astride the dish, just to satisfy him ; you can take care his legs or clothes do not go into the gravy.'

'Anything for a quiet life,' said the father. 'What does Limby want ?—Limby ride ? '

'Limby on bone !—Limby on meat ! '

'Shall I put him across ?' said Mr. Lumpy.

'Just for one moment,' said his mamma : 'it won't hurt the mutton.'

The father rose, and took Limby from his chair, and, with the greatest caution, held his son's

Limby Lumpy

legs astride, so that they might hang on each side of the dish without touching it ; 'just to satisfy him,' as he said, 'that they might dine in quiet,' and was about to withdraw him from it immediately.

But Limby was not to be cheated in that way, he wished to feel the saddle *under* him, and accordingly forced himself down upon it ; but feeling it rather warmer than was agreeable, started, and lost his balance, and fell down among the dishes, soused in melted butter, cauliflower, and gravy—floundering, and kicking, and screaming, to the detriment of glasses, jugs, dishes, and everything else on the table.

'My child ! my child !' said his mamma ; 'O ! save my child !'

She snatched him up, and pressed his begreased garments close to the bosom of her best silk gown.

Limby Lumpy

Neither father nor mother wanted any more dinner after this. As to Limby, he was as frisky afterwards as if nothing had happened ; and, about half an hour from the time of this disaster, *cried for his dinner*.

The Oyster Patties

The Oyster Patties

THERE was once a little boy, who
perhaps might have been a good
little fellow if his friends had taken
pains to make him so, but I do not
know how it was, instead of teaching him to be good, they gave him
everything he cried for ; so, whenever he wished to have anything, he
had only to cry ; and if he did not
get it directly, he cried louder and
louder till at last he got it. By
this means Alfred was not only very
naughty but very unhappy ; he was
crying from morning till night ; he
had no pleasure in anything ; he
was in everybody's way, and nobody

The Oyster Patties

liked to be with him. Well, one
day his mamma thought she would
give him a day of pleasure, and
make him very happy indeed, so
she told him he should have a feast,
and dine under the great cedar tree
that stood upon the lawn, and that
his cousins should be invited to dine
with him, and that he should have
whatever he chose for his dinner. So
she rang the bell, and she told the
servants to take out tables and chairs
and to lay the cloth upon the table
under the tree; and she ordered
her two footmen to be ready to
wait upon him. She desired the
butler to tell the cook to prepare
the dinner, and to get all sorts of
nice dishes for the feast; but she
said to Alfred, 'What shall you
like best of all, my dear boy?' So
Alfred tried to think of something
that he had never had before, and he

The Oyster Patties

recollected that one day he had heard a lady say, who was dining with his papa and mamma, that the oyster patties were the best she had ever eaten. Now Alfred had never tasted oyster patties, so he said he would have oyster patties for dinner. 'Oyster patties, my dear boy? You cannot have oyster patties at this time of the year, there are no oysters to be had,' his mamma said to him; 'try, love, to think of something else.'

But naughty Alfred said, 'No, I can think of nothing else,' so the cook was sent for, and desired to think of something that he might like as well. The cook proposed first a currant pie, then a barberry pie, or a codlin pie with custard. 'No, no, no,' said Alfred, shaking his head. 'Or a strawberry tart, my sweet boy; or apricot jam?'

The Oyster Patties

said his mamma, in a soothing tone of voice.

But Alfred said, 'No, mamma, no, I don't like strawberries; I don't like apricot jam; I want oysters.'

'But you cannot have oysters, my little master,' said the cook. 'But I will have oysters,' said the little boy, 'and you shan't say that I can't have them, shall she, mamma?' and he began to scream and to cry. 'Do not cry, my sweet soul,' said his mamma, 'and we will see what we can do; dry up your tears, my little man, and come with me, and the cook, I daresay, will be able to get some oysters before dinner; it is a long time to dinner, you know, and I have some pretty toys for you upstairs if you will come with me till dinner is ready.' So she took the little crying

The Oyster Patties

boy by the hand and led him up to her room, and she whispered to the cook as she passed not to say anything more about it now, and that she hoped he would forget the oyster patties by the time dinner was ready. In the meantime she took all the pains she could to amuse and please him, and as fast as he grew tired of one toy she brought out another. At last, after some hours, she gave him a beautiful toy for which she had paid fifteen shillings. It was a sand toy of a woman sitting at a spinning wheel, and when it was turned up the little figure began spinning away, and the wheel turned round and round as fast as if the woman who turned it had been alive. Alfred wanted to see how it was done, but, instead of going to his mother to ask her if she would be so good as to explain it to him, he began pulling it to pieces to look behind it. For some time he was very busy, and he had just succeeded in opening the large box at the back of the figure when all the sand that was in it came pouring out upon the floor, and when he tried to make the little woman spin again, he found she would not do it any more; she could not, for it was the sand dropping down that had made her move before.

Now do you know that Alfred was so very silly that he began to be angry even with the toy, and he said, 'Spin, I say; spin directly,' and then he shook it very hard, but in vain; the little hands did not move, and the wheel stood still. So then he was very angry indeed, and, setting up a loud cry, he threw the toy to the other end of

The Oyster Patties

the room. Just at this very moment
the servant opened the door and
said that dinner was ready and that
Alfred's cousins were arrived.

'Come, my dear child, you are
tired of your toys, I see,' said
mamma, 'so come to dinner, darling;
it is all ready, under the tree.' So
away they went, leaving the room
all strewed with toys, with broken
pieces, and the sand all spilt in a
heap upon the floor. When they
went under the dark spreading
branches of the fine old cedar tree,
there they saw the table covered
with dishes and garnished with
flowers; there were chickens, and
ham, and tongue, and lobsters,
besides tarts, and custards, and
jellies, and cakes, and cream, and
I do not know how many nice
things besides; there was Alfred's
high chair at the head of the table,

The Oyster Patties

and he was soon seated in it, as master of the feast, with his mother sitting by him, his cousins opposite to him, his nurse standing on the other side, and the two footmen waiting besides. As soon as his cousins were helped to what they liked best, his mamma said, 'What will you eat first, Alfred, my love? A wing of a chicken?' 'No,' said Alfred, pushing it away. 'A slice of ham, darling?' said nurse. 'No,' said Alfred, in a louder tone. 'A little bit of lobster, my dear?' 'No, no,' replied the naughty boy. 'Well, what *will* you have then?' said his mother, who was almost tired of him. 'I will have oyster patties,' said he. 'That is the only thing you cannot have, my love, you know, so do not think of it any more, but taste a bit of this pie; I am sure you will like it.'

The Oyster Patties

'You *said* I should have oyster patties by dinner time,' said Alfred, 'and so I will have nothing else.' 'I am sorry you are such a sad naughty child,' said his mother; 'I thought you would have been so pleased with all these nice things to eat.' 'They are *not* nice,' said the child, who was not at all grateful for all that his mother had done, but was now in such a passion, that he took the piece of currant tart, which his nurse again offered to him, and squeezing up as much as his two little hands could hold, he threw it at his nurse, and stained her nice white handkerchief and apron with the red juice. Just at this moment his papa came into the garden, and walked up to the table. 'What is all this?' said he. 'Alfred, you seem to be a very naughty boy,

The Oyster Patties

indeed; and I must tell you, sir, I shall allow this no longer; get down from your chair, sir, and beg your nurse's pardon.' Alfred had hardly ever heard his father speak so before, and he felt so frightened, that he left off crying, and did as he was bid. Then his father took him by the hand, and led him away. His mother said she was sure he would now be good, and eat the currant tart. But his papa said, 'No, no, it is now too late, he must come with me'; so he led him away, without saying another word. He took him into the village, and he stopped at the door of a poor cottage.

'May we come in?' said his father. 'Oh yes, and welcome,' said a poor woman, who was standing at a table with a saucepan in her hand. 'What are you

The Oyster Patties

doing, my good woman?' 'Only putting out the children's supper, your honour.' 'And what have you got for their supper?' 'Only some potatoes, please you, sir, but they be nicely boiled, and here come the hungry boys! They are coming in from their work, and they will soon make an end of them, I warrant.'

As she said these words, in came John, and William, and Thomas, all with rosy cheeks and smiling faces. They sat down, one on a wooden stool, one on a broken chair, and one on the corner of the table, and they all began to eat the potatoes very heartily. But Alfred's papa said, 'Stop, my good boys, do not eat any more, but come with me.' The boys stared, but their mother told them to do as they were bid, so they

The Oyster Patties

left off eating, and followed the
gentleman. Alfred and his papa
walked on till they arrived once
more under the cedar tree in the
garden, and there was the fine
feast, all standing just as they had
left it, for Alfred's cousins were
gone away, and his mamma would
not have the dinner taken away,
because she hoped that Alfred
would come back to it. 'Now,
boys,' said the gentleman, 'you
may all sit down to this table, and
eat whatever you like.'

John, William, and Thomas sat
down as quickly as they could, and
began to devour the chickens and
tarts, and all the good things at a
great rate ; and Alfred, who now
began to be very hungry, would
gladly have been one of the party ;
but when he was going to sit down,
his papa said, 'No, sir, this feast is

The Oyster Patties

not for *you;* there is nothing here
that you like to eat, you know ; so
you will wait upon these boys, if
you please, who seem as if they
would find plenty that they will
like.' Alfred at this began to cry
again, and said he wanted to go to
his mamma ; but his father did not
mind his crying, and said he should
not go to his mamma again till he
was quite a good boy. 'So now, sir,
hand this bread to John, and now
take a clean plate to Thomas, and
now stand ready to carry this custard
to William. There now, wait till
they have all done.' It was of no
use now to cry or scream ; he was
obliged to do it all. When the
boys had quite finished their supper,
they went home, and Alfred was
led by his father into the house.
Before he went to bed, a cup of
milk and water and a piece of

The Oyster Patties

brown bread were put before him,
and his father said, ' That is your
supper, Alfred.' Alfred began to
cry again, and said he did not
want such a supper as that. ' Very
well,' said his father, ' then go to
bed without, and it shall be saved
for your breakfast.' Alfred cried
and screamed louder than ever ;
so his father ordered the maid to
put him to bed. When he was in
bed, he thought his mamma would
come and see him, and bring him
something nice, and he lay awake
a long while ; but she did not come,
and he cried and cried till at last
he fell asleep.

In the morning when he awoke
he was so hungry he could hardly
wait to be dressed, but asked for
his breakfast every minute. When
he saw the maid bring in the brown
bread again without any butter, and

The Oyster Patties

some milk and water, he was very near crying again ; but he thought if he did he should perhaps lose his breakfast as he had lost his supper ; so he checked his tears, and ate a hearty meal.

'Well,' said his father, who came into the room just as he was eating the last bit of bread. 'I am glad to see the little boy who could not yesterday find anything good enough for him at a feast eating such simple fare as this so heartily. Come, Alfred, now you may come to your dear mamma.'

THE END

Printed by R. & R. CLARK, LIMITED, *Edinburgh*